Oliver's Travels in Space

Written and Illustrated by
Kristie A. Zweig

I dedicate this book to my son Kyle, and to all the dreamers, astronomers, and stargazers in the world.

Oliver loves to dream
of traveling through space.

One night when he went to sleep,
this was the case.

YES! Outer Space!

He woke up to see
all the planets and Sun.

He thought to himself,
"Oh my, what fun!"

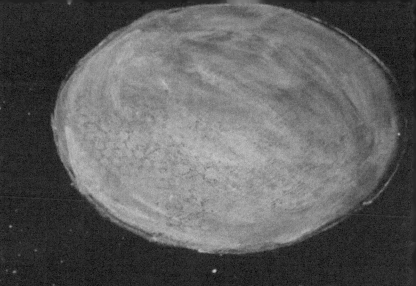

I will soar through the air
and all the planets I will see.

I will fly faster than a bird
or maybe a bee.

The Sun was too hot
to visit that day.

Oliver moved on to
Mercury as he went
on his way.

Tiny Mercury

Venus was next and looked very yellow.

Oliver said Hello with a very large bellow.

As he flew through the air,
he came to our home.

Earth was beautiful,
a blue and green dome.

Our home Earth!

Oliver next saw a beautiful sight.

A tiny red planet called Mars in the night.

Appearing next is
Jupiter which was
enormous!

It reminded him
of a huge Brontosaurus.

Jupiter

Saturn with it's rings was
next to be.

What a sight that was
for him to see!

Saturn
Wow!

A smaller planet
called Uranus came
into view.

It was greenish and
had tiny rings too.

Uranus

The last planet finally
was in view.

It was Neptune and
it was very, very blue.

Oliver was very tired
from his travels and said ,
"What an adventure I've
had!" "Wow, I'm back
in my bed."

A wonderful journey,
as it would seem.

Oliver never forgot
his wonderful dream!

Starting after the Sun, Oliver traveled from Mercury to Neptune.

Let's see if you can find all the planets including the Sun and the Moon.

About the Author/Illustrator

Kristie has worked in an Elementary School for many years and enjoys writing and painting. She retired last year and finally has the time to do what she loves most, creating stories for children. This book is about a little boy named Oliver. He dreams of space and the planets and would love to travel there. There is something about the vast, beautiful night sky that people have marveled at since creation. Oliver does journey there and visits each planet. I hope you enjoy his story and will learn about the planets. Kristie's previous books in print are:

'The Adventures of Finneas Frog'
'Believe Without Seeing'

Ingram Content Group UK Ltd.
Milton Keynes UK
UKHW050645260323
419121UK00003B/49